Friday Afternoon Fun

Story by Julie Ellis
Illustrations by Naomi C. Lewis

Contents

Chapter 1	The Running Race	2
Chapter 2	The Egg and Spoon Race	8
Chapter 3	The Sack Race	12

HOUGHTON MIFFLIN HARCOURT
Supplemental Publishers

www.Rigby.com
800-531-5015

Chapter 1

The Running Race

Emma and Matthew looked over
at the parents who were standing
by the track.
They saw their mother waving to them.

"Hi, Mom!" called Emma. "I'm glad you came."

"I'm going to win this race!" shouted Matthew.

The Running Race

3

Friday Afternoon Fun

Everyone in the class got ready
for the first race.

"Catch me if you can!" Matthew said to Emma.
He knew that he was the fastest runner
in the class.

"Ready... set... **go!**" called the teacher.

The children ran down the track
as fast as they could.

Soon Matthew was in front.

Emma tried very hard.
She ran past three children.
Now the only one in front of her was Matthew.

The Running Race

Matthew looked back.
He was surprised to see Emma
so close behind him.

Emma kept looking ahead,
and she ran past Matthew
just as they got to the finish line.

The Running Race

"Good running," said Mom, giving them a hug.

Emma was very happy,
but Matthew was not happy with himself.

Chapter 2
The Egg and Spoon Race

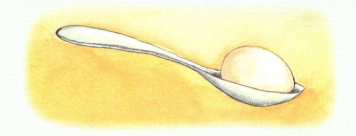

"It's the egg and spoon race now," said Emma. "You could win this one, Matthew."

"I'm not running in any more races today," said Matthew.

"Races are not about being first," said Mom. "They are about trying hard and having fun."

"Come on, Matthew," said Emma. "The egg and spoon race will be fun."

The Egg and Spoon Race

"All right," he said. "I'll give it a try. I might beat you this time."

9

Friday Afternoon Fun

The children lined up.

"Ready... set... **go!**" called the teacher.

Matthew walked fast,
but he was very careful.
He kept watching the egg on his spoon.

Emma tried to run past him.
But the egg on her spoon started to wobble,
and it fell off.

"Well done, Matthew," said Mom
as he crossed the line first.
"I'm proud of you for giving it a try."

The Egg and Spoon Race

Chapter 3

The Sack Race

Then the teacher called out,
"It's time for the parents' race!"

"Go on, Mom," said Emma.

"No," said Mom.
"I can't run fast like you two."

The Sack Race

Friday Afternoon Fun

"You can do it, Mom!" said Emma.
"You might win because this is a sack race."

"Races are not about always being first,"
said Matthew with a big smile.
"They are about trying hard and having fun."

Mom laughed. "All right," she said.
"I'll give it a try."

The Sack Race

Friday Afternoon Fun

"Go, Mom!" shouted Matthew and Emma.

Mom tried hard, but she fell over because she was laughing so much.

"Don't worry, Mom!" said Matthew. "We're proud of you!"